A Lyon in Her Bed

The Lyon's Den Connected World

USA Today Bestselling Author

Amanda Mariel

ARE YOU SIGNED UP FOR DRAGONBLADE'S BLOG?

You'll get the latest news and information on exclusive giveaways, exclusive excerpts, coming releases, sales, free books, cover reveals and more.

Check out our complete list of authors, too!

No spam, no junk. That's a promise!

Sign Up Here

www.dragonbladepublishing.com

Dearest Reader;

Thank you for your support of a small press. At Dragonblade Publishing, we strive to bring you the highest quality Historical Romance from the some of the best authors in the business. Without your support, there is no 'us', so we sincerely hope you adore these stories and find some new favorite authors along the way.

Happy Reading!

CEO, Dragonblade Publishing

Additional Dragonblade books by Author Amanda Mariel

The Lyon's Den Connected World
A Lyon in Her Bed

Wolfbane Books
Love's Legacy
One Wanton Wager
Forever in Your Arms

Other Lyon's Den Books
Into the Lyon's Den by Jade Lee
The Scandalous Lyon by Maggi Andersen
Fed to the Lyon by Mary Lancaster
The Lyon's Lady Love by Alexa Aston
The Lyon's Laird by Hildie McQueen
The Lyon Sleeps Tonight by Elizabeth Ellen Carter

CHAPTER 1

London, 1814

L EONARD, LEO QUINTON, sixth Earl of Morton, needed an heir. Since one could not beget an heir without a wife, he devised a plan.

His plan was a sure way to secure a wife without the need for courtship, false promises, and betrayal. It was perfect, for it would keep his heart unattached.

He'd had more than his fill of tender feelings, and he'd not subject himself again. Not for any reason. He could not, would not, ever give his heart away as he had once before.

The pains of his past gnawed at him as he made his way into the Lyon's Den for an audience with the infamous Black Widow of Whitehall, Mrs. Bessie Dove-Lyon.

If anyone could find him a wife quickly, she could. The widow would undoubtedly have several candidates with slightly scandalous backgrounds but excellent bloodlines for him to choose from.

A perfect solution to be sure.

A simple arrangement to benefit them both. She gives him an heir, and he gives her his title and protection—the end.

No one gets hurt, no one gets betrayed, and everyone gets what they want.

He entered the blue building at the end of Cleveland Row, then strode across the gentlemen's entry and up the stairs leading to Mrs. Dove-Lyon's private parlor.

His confidence never waned. He was doing the right thing. This was the fastest, most straightforward way to secure what he needed.

And he would get what he sought.

One of Dove-Lyon's men stepped in front of her parlor door, blocking Leo's entrance, as he approached. A hulking man who now scowled at Leo. "State your business," the man demanded.

Leo gave a relaxed grin. "I am here to see Mrs. Dove-Lyon."

"She is presently occupied."

Leo leaned his shoulder against the wall outside of the office. "I'll wait," he said with cool defiance.

"Perhaps you would like to enjoy a game of faro? Kindly give me your name, and when she is available, I will send for you." He wasn't really making a suggestion and took a menacing step toward Leo.

Leo did not flinch. His business here was too important, and the gaming tables held no appeal. He'd come for one reason, to secure a wife. He'd not find his future countess at the tables. "My name is Lord Morton, and I will remain where I am."

Before the guard could do anything, Mrs. Dove-Lyon's door swung open.

A tiny woman with unremarkable brown hair and eyes strode into the hallway before drawing to a stop to stare at the men blocking her path. She met Leo's gaze and said, "Excuse me."

He ought to have moved aside and allowed her passage. Instead, he studied her, trailing his gaze over her oval-shaped face, slender shoulders, and small breasts.

She was no beauty. Still, she was pleasant enough. "What is your name?" he asked.

Her gaze turned curious, and she said, "Miss Hawthorne. Miss Emeline Hawthorn, to be precise."

"And your sire?" Leo continued.

The woman narrowed her eyes. "Was a physician."

"Then, you have good breeding."

She gave a slow nod.

Caution, mixed with something else entirely, shone in her eyes. A spark of something more lively. Could it be hope? Had this woman come here searching for a spouse, too?

Leo stepped closer to her. She could be the answer to his quest.

Just then, Mrs. Dove-Lyon stepped into the doorway of her parlor to gaze out at them. "If you wish an audience, you may enter. Otherwise, allow the woman to pass. She hasn't the coin to pay for my services."

This was bloody perfect! The woman had indeed come seeking a match. What's more, she was desperate and met his requirements.

This was a woman of good breeding, one who undoubtedly faced ruin over a lack of finances. Best of all, he had what she sought.

Leo turned back to Miss Hawthorne. "You will do nicely."

Her eyes rounded. "Do for what, exactly?"

"I think it safe to assume that you came here to procure a husband." He laid his hand on his chest, his fingers fanned out over his cravat. "As it happens, I have come for a wife."

Miss Hawthorne stared at him, her eyes wide. "Are you proposing marriage?"

"I am," Leo smoothed his jacket.

"This is not how it works," Mrs. Dove-Lyon protested.

Leo turned a charming smile on the widow. "I'll pay your fee."

She nodded, then stepped to the side to allow entrance into her parlor. "Come in," her gaze went from Leo to Miss Hawthorne, "both of you. There is no need to air your laundry in the hall."

Leo waited several long moments for Miss Hawthorne to move. Just when he thought she might bolt, the woman nodded, then strolled into the parlor.

He followed, and once inside, turned to face her. As the door clicked shut, he said, "We can wed at once."

"Why?" Emeline asked, her brows drawing together as she tried to understand what was happening. Perhaps he was a madman? Something had to be amiss.

She wet her lips, then asked, "Why should you wish to marry me? A stranger. And so soon at that?"

"I know what I need to know." He held one finger up. "You are in want of a wealthy husband." He held up another finger. "I happen to be exceedingly wealthy and titled."

Could fate be smiling on her? She cared not about titles. However, she did need a financially stable husband. That is precisely why she'd come to the Lyon's Den.

Mother meant to marry her off to a baron nearly three times her age in order to save them. Her stomach turned at the thought, disgust rising in her. Madman or not, the gentleman standing before her was far closer to her age and quite handsome, too.

If she must marry for necessity, she saw no reason why she shouldn't at least have a husband around her own age. One who she could bed without revulsion.

Still... She nibbled her lip, bringing her gaze back to his. "And what would you stand to gain from me?"

"A legitimate heir." He stepped closer, still smiling. "I am the Earl of Morton. As my wife, you will be a countess. I'll give you a generous allowance and run of my estates. In return, I want unrestricted access to your bed."

She could not stifle the cynical laughter that bubbled up in her. This man was just too much. Her shoulders shook as her laugh rang out, filling the hall. "And once you have finished with me? What then?"

"You will have your freedom. You can live in whichever of my homes you choose, your allowance will remain, and you will continue to enjoy your position as my countess. I will bother you no more. All I ask is that you use discretion if you take a lover."

Dare she accept? Emeline wasn't sure. It seemed too good to be true. Yet, here he stood, a flesh and blood earl, offering her precisely what she sought. All he asked in return was the same thing any husband would expect of her.

Mrs. Dove-Lyon pressed a teacup into her hand. "Drink," she ordered.

Emeline took a sip of the brew, then cringed. "What is in this drink?"

"Whisky-laced tea, my dear. Just enough to settle your nerves."

Emeline set the cup on a nearby table. She turned back to the earl and squared her shoulders. "I will agree, with one additional condition."

Curiosity filled his grey eyes. "Go on."

"You must agree to provide for my mother, too."

"Consider it done." He turned to Mrs. Dove-Lyon, then reached into his jacket and retrieved a velvet pouch. "Your fee."

She nodded as she accepted the pouch. Turning her gaze back on Emeline, she said, "You have made a wise choice."

Despite Dove-Lyon's assurance, Emeline could not help but wonder if she had indeed made the right choice. Regardless, marriage to this man would suit her exceedingly better than the elderly man Mother had chosen for her. She forced a smile. "Thank you."

"We will marry today at my residence. Bring your mother if you would like." Lord Morton moved to the door. "Number twenty-six, Grosvenor Square. Be there by five of the clock."

Emeline swallowed back the uncertainty welling within her. If she would be sold like chattel, she might as well be the one in charge of the auction. She nodded. "As you wish."

Those three simple words—as you wish—sealed her fate.

Pray, let it be for the better.

CHAPTER 2

"**M**OTHER, I AM to wed the Earl of Morton," Emeline announced the moment she returned home.

Mother looked up from her needlepoint and scowled. "What game is this? You are to marry the baron."

"It is not a game, I assure you. Lord Morton has offered for me, and I have accepted." She averted her gaze to the worn floorboards. They'd sold the rugs that once covered them last week. They had sold the paintings a week earlier and their jewelry two weeks prior to that. Her stomach clenched at just how far they had fallen since Father's death.

"No," Mother said, her voice stern.

Emeline sucked in a breath. The sharp edge in her tone cut like a blade. She came further into the drawing room, her back stiff and chin notched. "I am three and twenty. Nearly a spinster, and certainly of an age to make my own choice." She stared into Mother's deep brown eyes, so much like her own. "I will marry Lord Morton at five of the clock. Should you wish to be present, you will need to hurry. We must look our best."

She pivoted, then strode toward the hallway, intent to go to her room and make ready.

"Wait. Emeline, come back here," her mother demanded.

Emeline turned to find her striding after her. Before her mother could say anything else, Emeline spoke, "I will marry him. There is nothing you can do to change my mind."

She seemed to soften. "How can you be sure his offer is true? Where did you meet this Lord Morton? I've not heard his name before."

Emeline's pulse thrummed as she considered how to answer the barrage of questions. It would displease her mother to learn Emeline had gone to the Lyon's Den, but she could not hide the fact.

Not even for the sake of her feelings.

Emeline would have to be honest. "I went to the Lyon's Den to call upon Mrs. Dove-Lyon."

"You didn't!" She brought her hand to her chest. "You're ruined! No one will have you now. Not after you set foot in such an unsavory place."

"No, you are wrong. Lord Morton will have me. I will be a countess."

"Rubbish! You have no funds to pay the matchmaking fee." Mother stared at her, her concern deepening as evidenced by the deep lines etching her face. "Our name will be drug through the mud."

Emeline grinned, for she now had the upper hand. "Lord Morton paid the fee," she said.

"You do not find that peculiar? What do you know of this lord?" She rested her hand on Emeline's upper arm. "He could be scandalous, a wastrel given to drink. A rake or criminal. Marrying him could make our situation far worse."

Emeline gave a slight shake of her head. "He wants an heir without having to engage his heart or his time in properly wooing a wife. He's offered me a generous allowance and the run of his houses." She stared deep into her mother's eyes, hoping she'd understand. "He has also agreed to provide for you. He is wealthy and titled. Our problems are over."

"The baron is wealthy and titled, too. What's more, we know him. He's an upstanding gentleman and fond of you." Mother twisted her hands together. "What will he think? I've already promised you to him."

"He is older than Father was. Nearly three times my age. I cannot…will not marry him."

"Be sensible. The baron would give you a pleasant life."

She squeezed her mother's hands. "I am being reasonable." As she made haste for the stairs, she called over her shoulder, "Be ready by three, or I will go alone. I shan't be late for my own wedding."

Emeline did not bother to look back. She hoped her mother would accompany her, but in the end, it mattered not. She would marry Lord Morton. He was the perfect solution.

Well, maybe not perfect, but he was her choice. The earl was a man who would not betray her. One who was forthcoming with what he desired. A man of her own age.

Yes, it would be a marriage of convenience—a business arrangement where they both stood to gain what they wanted without risking their hearts. Emeline had once hoped for love, but that was long ago. Her current circumstances called for a practical match. Love did not matter, and she'd stopped wishing for it when reality taught her how fleeting the sentiment could be.

That wish had been before her heart was torn asunder. It was before her soul had been shredded to ribbons by a smooth-talking rogue.

Emeline shook the thoughts away. She could do without love. She'd have to, for it was not part of the agreement she'd made with the earl.

Give him an heir, then move into a different residence and take up a separate life from her husband, just as he wished.

She would live out the rest of her days without fear of poverty. What's more, she'd live those years on her own terms.

She'd have her child for company, and make friends with nearby neighbors. Lord Morton would have to come around occasionally. He'd have an interest in his son and his property. God willing, she and her husband would develop a friendship. But if they did not, she would carry on despite it.

Surely, Emeline made the right choice. If nothing else, she'd made the *only* choice she could tolerate. After all, no gentlemen were calling save for the baron. There most certainly weren't any princes coming to whisk her away.

She had to save herself.

And so, she would.

The carriage ride to Mayfair passed in silence. Though Emeline turned her attention to her mother from time to time, neither spoke.

When they arrived at Lord Morton's impressive residence, Mother turned to Emeline, her eyes wide. "It is a stately home. Perhaps you have done well."

Emeline smiled as the butler admitted them to the grand home. As a footman took their cloaks, the earl appeared in the entry hall. His gaze met hers, and he nodded. "I will send a footman for your trunks."

"I did not think to have them brought along."

"Then provide your address. I will send someone to fetch your things."

Why hadn't Emeline thought to pack? Of course, he would wish for her to sleep here. She would be his wife by nightfall. He'd want to come to her bed. How else were they to make a baby? And when one considered the terms of their agreement, it was Emeline's only duty.

He'd have no wish to delay on that score.

"First, I shall see the marriage contract," Mother said, stepping forward.

"Of course. Right this way." Lord Morton led them into a richly appointed parlor decorated in mahogany wood and deep blue velvets. He indicated a carved wood table. "Peruse away, Mrs. Hawthorne. I am certain you will agree I have been generous."

"Indeed," she said, then moved to take up the stack of parchment.

Lord Morton turned to Emeline. "You will need to sign the agreement."

She bobbed her head in understanding.

"Once you have, we will get on with the ceremony." He glanced across the room.

Emeline followed his glance to find a vicar seated near an enormous window, a bible resting on his lap.

Beside the vicar sat a plump woman dressed in purple. Perhaps his wife? It would seem Lord Morton thought of everything.

"Very well," Emeline said before moving to stand beside her mother.

She took up the quill from the table and waited as her mother read. There would be no reason for Emeline to read the contract herself.

If anything were out of order, Mother would be sure to discover the error and point it out to Lord Morton for correction.

After what seemed to be an excruciatingly long time, her mother set the last page back on the table and turned to Lord Morton. "Very generous, indeed. You have exceeded my expectations, my lord. It is with a happy heart I give you my daughter."

"Then let us get on with it," the earl turned his smile to Emeline and gave an encouraging nod. "It is what we discussed. You have your choice of residence once I have an heir and an allowance of fifteen pounds a month. I have also provided for your mother. Furthermore, I have set up a jointure in the case that I leave you a widow."

"Go on, dearest," Mother encouraged. "There is no reason to stall." She waved toward the contract. "Time is wasting."

Emeline's hand shook as she dipped the quill in the inkwell. An image of the baron flashed through her mind, and her determination returned. Lord Morton was a far better match, come what may.

She scrolled her name on the contract, sealing the bargain.

Turning back to the room at large, she met the earl's gaze.

She forced a smile, then walked across the plush carpeting to stand beside him. Mother and the other woman stood nearby as the vicar stared at her and the earl, bible in hand.

"We are gathered here today, before God, to join this couple in holy matrimony," the vicar began.

Emeline drew in a steadying breath as she studied Lord Morton. In a matter of minutes, she would become his wife. In a matter of hours, she would share his bed.

If all went accordingly, in mere months, she would give birth to his heir.

She stared into his cool, grey eyes and wondered if there might be more between them. As she spoke her vows, a small spark of hope ignited deep within her.

Perhaps she could fall in love with him, and just maybe, he could come to love her back.

CHAPTER 3

"**I** NOW PRONOUNCE you man and wife…"

Leo nodded to the vicar. "Thank you." A weight had been lifted from his shoulders at having the ceremony done. He had worried that Miss Hawthorne, or rather Emeline, now Lady Morton, would change her mind.

It came as a great relief that there would be no backing out now.

"Won't you kiss your bride?" Mrs. Hawthorne asked.

Leo turned to his new mother-in-law and gave a tight grin. "I would hate to scandalize my countess."

Emeline took a tentative step toward him. "I would not object."

He met her gaze and noticed for the first time how extraordinary her eyes were. Honey-gold rims circled what he'd thought were dull brown irises.

His gut tightened at the warmth reflecting within them. Was it for him?

One kiss. He could manage one quick brush of his lips to hers. Once he had done with it, he would save any further intimate gestures for the bedchamber where they belonged.

He inhaled a steadying breath, bracing himself. "If it will please you," he said, stepping closer before pressing his lips to hers.

A bolt of longing shot straight from the place their lips joined, to his cock. Bedding his new wife would be no chore at all. In fact, he was rather looking forward to burying himself within her sweet little body.

He lingered a moment longer than he'd intended as desire suffused him, then pulled away with all haste.

Kissing her proved dangerous. To his dismay, more than his male anatomy had responded to the touch of her lips. If he were not careful, he might find his heart engaged.

And that was not to be born.

Not under any circumstance.

He pivoted, his gaze returning to the vicar. "Let us conclude our business."

"As you wish, my lord," the vicar closed his bible.

After the vicar had gone, and the housekeeper had arrived, Leo addressed his wife. "She will show you to your chamber. You can expect me to visit within a few hours."

"Very well." She brushed a kiss to her mother's cheek. "I will see you soon, Mother."

"Not too soon, I suspect. It is your honeymoon, after all." Mrs. Hawthorne pulled Emeline into her embrace. "I believe you have done well, dearest. I'll see that your things arrive straight away. Do not fret for me. Your earl has been exceedingly generous on that count."

Mrs. Hawthorne curtsied to Leo, then took her leave.

A moment later, Emeline followed the housekeeper out, leaving him alone in the parlor.

Leo released a pent-up breath as he poured a tumbler of scotch. If that kiss was anything to judge by, he had gotten more than he'd bargained for in his new countess.

The fact unsettled him more than he cared to admit and caused him to hesitate going to her. He needed a bit of time to clear his head first.

He tipped the glass back, drinking the contents in one long draw. The warmth from the liquor spread through him, easing his concern as it blazed a pleasant trail down his throat.

She was but a woman, and he well knew how to handle them. There was nothing to fear, for he could withstand emotional entanglement. Distance—emotional distance—would be vital. He could manage that while keeping his heart closed off.

Leo would get her with child as quickly as possible. Then he would pack her off to the country. His countess would raise the babe until the time came for him to take over.

This marriage was nothing more than a business arrangement, and he would do well to treat it as such.

He would be kind. Show her the respect his countess deserved and care for her needs. But under no circumstances would he attempt to romance her.

He most certainly would not lower his guard, and there would be no more kissing. Not on the mouth, at any rate.

EMELINE SAT IN front of the vanity in her bedchamber, dressed in nothing more than her shift. She glanced at the bed across from her with its white curtains and carved cherry-wood posts. The earl would soon come to claim her. Together they would lie in that bed and join their bodies.

The thought sent excitement through her. She was not afraid of the act of lovemaking. Still, she had always imagined that when she wed, she'd do so for love.

How could she bare herself for a man she scarcely knew? Would he be gentle with her? Would she find enjoyment in the act?

Mother told her that many women did, and Emeline prayed she'd be one of them.

She feathered her fingers over her lips, recalling the kiss he'd given her a few hours ago. Her lips tingled, even now, and she hoped he would kiss her again.

Perhaps their marriage of convenience could blossom into one of love?

The door swung open, her husband filling the frame. He wore a dark blue banyan, loosely tied and draping to reveal a section of his muscular chest. Her pulse thrummed as she brought her gaze up to meet his.

"Countess," he said with a slight bow of his head as he entered and closed the door behind him.

"My lord," she replied. Now that he was here, she felt as anxious as a newborn colt.

Mercy, he was handsome. And imposing. From his sandy hair to his chiseled jaw and broad shoulders, all the way to his large feet.

He could easily overpower her. Take what he pleased from her, even her heart, and leave her in shambles.

And yet, she found him altogether appealing. Her fingers itched to touch his bronzed skin, and at the same time, common sense told her to be cautious.

He held out a hand. "Join me in bed."

Her eyes rounded. "I thought we might spend a little time becoming familiar with one another before…" her words trailed off, her gaze returning to the bed. "That is, I had wine sent up. I thought we might enjoy a glass first."

He cast his gaze around the chamber, then brought it back to her, one brow arched. "Where is it?"

"In my sitting room." She stood. "Please join me." Emeline headed toward the door that joined her bedchamber to her personal sitting room.

Relief sailed through her when she heard the fall of his footsteps trailing behind her.

She sat on the settee by the window, then reached for the wine decanter on the side table. After pouring two glasses, she held one out to him.

A flicker of annoyance flashed through his blue-grey eyes, but he took the offered wine and joined her on the settee.

Emeline took a long sip for fortification, then angled her body toward his. "It is not lost on me that we should have explored this subject further before the wedding. Nonetheless, it cannot be ignored."

"What subject do you refer to?"

"The terms of our marriage." She stiffened in an effort to appear far more confident than she felt. "I understand my duty. I am to give you an heir, and to do so, I must bed you. However, I must admit to being surprised when you sent me to my room and left me to dine alone."

His expression turned speculative. "Is it your wish to dine together?"

"I believe it best that we come to know each other, my lord. If we are to raise a child together, we should, at the least, be friendly with one another. There will be times when we have to cooperate for the child's sake."

He crossed his ankle over his thigh and studied her. "You will see to the child until he comes of an age to learn his duties to the title. After that, I will take over. As I told you before, your obligation to me will end once you deliver a son. You need not spend any more time with me. I have several houses. You can reside in whichever you choose and live your life as you please."

"Even so, there will be circumstances that require our paths to cross. Occasions when we must be in each other's company." She took another drink, her tongue darting out to lick the wine from her lips. "It would be best if we got along. Don't you agree?"

"Perhaps." He swirled the red liquid in his glass as he studied her. "What did you have in mind?"

She smiled, her anxiety easing a bit. "To start, I would like to share meals."

"I will join you for the evening meal but will take my breakfast and noontime meals alone."

Emeline fought the urge to argue and nodded. "Very well. We dine together each night and spend two hours together every afternoon."

"No." Lord Morton shook his head.

"No?" Emeline stared at him. "Surely you can spare two hours. They need not be in the afternoon, but I do require them."

He sighed and brought the glass back to his lips. "I can spare one." His gaze turned hard, uncompromising. "One hour each afternoon."

A minor victory, but she would hold on to it. "I suppose that will have to suffice."

"Good," he said, then drained the contents of his glass. "I will see you tomorrow at two of the clock." He stood. "Meet me in the garden for a walk."

The shock caused her to bolt to her feet. "You are leaving?"

"I realize you are not ready to consummate our union. I will grant you one day to rectify that."

Emeline could not find her voice. Even if she could, she had no idea what to say. The last thing she had expected was for the earl to leave her a virgin on their wedding night.

Perhaps his hasty departure should please her? His actions showed that he had a care for her feelings. After all, he was giving her time to grow more comfortable. But then, maybe she had it all wrong and should be upset. Perhaps his actions showed a distaste for her rather than caring. Maybe she was not to his liking.

He reached the door, then turned back to face her. He trailed his gaze down her body, pausing at her breasts before continuing lower.

A hot flush spread across her cheeks. Their eyes met, and she noted the unmistakable passion in his gaze.

A coy smile curled her lips, and she said, "Tomorrow, my lord."

CHAPTER 4

H E MUST BE addled to have agreed to her foolish demands, Leo thought as his gaze raked over his countess. Out here in the garden with the sun casting her in warm light, he truly saw her for the first time. The woman he'd thought rather plain was actually quite remarkable.

Golden streaks shot through her brown hair that had appeared dull at first sight, and her pale skin held a hint of peach. Those soft brown eyes contained deep emotions and undeniable mystery.

Leo most liked her understated curves. Her breasts rounded and peeked out from the lace edging of her bodice, while her gown fitted nicely over the gentle swell of her hips and bottom.

His wife was anything but plain. In truth, she was delectable. A tiny treat he could scarcely wait to devour.

If he were not careful, for she was the sort of woman that inspired men, he would get trapped into feeling something for her, perhaps tenderness and more. The sort of emotions that made men want to protect her—the kind of woman that a man could not help but love.

Panic tightened his chest. She was the very sort that often brought a man to his knees. She could destroy him and leave him brokenhearted.

Leo would not allow her an inch where his heart was concerned. Though he fully intended to enjoy ravishing her.

"I grew up in Kent. As you know, my father was a physician. Mother cared for me while Father was about his work." Lady Morton looped her hand through his elbow. "I liked Sundays best as a girl. That was the one day each week that my father spent at home. We would attend church, then he would take me to the village pastry shop and buy me whatever I wished for. After, we would return home and spent time together out of doors if the weather permitted. If not, we would play games inside. Father, Mother, and me."

Her chest rose and fell as she took a breath before turning her smile on him. Leo's gaze returned to her chest as she started speaking again.

"Now, you know a bit about me. Tell me something about you? About your childhood?"

"I would rather not."

"Why?" She arched a questioning brow. "How else are we to get to know one another?"

"Very well," he conceded, then searched for something unimportant to share. "My favorite treat was lemon cream."

"I suppose that is a start." She shook her head. "Come now, tell me something more substantial."

He turned her down a path of thick shrubbery and flowering bushes. The last thing he wanted to do was share intimate details of his life with her. It was too dangerous to do so. Opening his past, his emotions…would lead nowhere good.

"What was your favorite thing to do as a boy?" she pressed.

Leo blew out a slow breath. "I enjoyed fishing."

"Do you still?"

He met her gaze, and the curiosity reflected within her eyes tugged at something deep within him. She seemed to have a genuine interest in him. Leo quickly averted his gaze. "When I have the time to indulge myself, I do."

She was quiet as he led her further into the garden, and Leo was grateful for the silence.

When she spoke again, her question unsettled him.

"What of your family? Do you have siblings?"

His heart squeezed, his throat tightening. It was a subject he had no desire to broach. One that stabbed too deep.

As he searched for a way to avoid answering, the rustling of a nearby bush caught his attention. "How peculiar," he said as he freed his arm from her hold.

He strode toward the rustling bush, then stilled as a mew reverberated from its depth. It would seem that somewhere within the hedge, a cat struggled to free itself.

"He's stuck." Lady Morton bent down to study the creature. "He's gotten his leg tangled in the branches."

Leo knelt beside her. "Don't fret," he said in a soothing tone, as much to her as to the small white and gray kitten.

He reached into the bush and pulled the offending branches apart. The kitten wriggled out, then faltered. It flopped onto its side and started licking the paw they'd freed.

He stroked the kitten between the ears. "Let us have a look, shall we?" he said as he took a paw into his hand and smoothed down the length of it. Nothing felt out of place, so he leaned in to have a closer look at the leg.

Lady Morton bent closer, her head next to his. The scent of orange blossom wafted from his wife, filling Leo's nose. He fought the sudden urge to steal a kiss.

Lord, she was sweet.

In an effort to distract himself, he focused on the kitten. A thorn stuck out from the one black toe pad on the kitten's foot. He held the paw as she reached out and plucked the offending thorn out. "There now," he soothed.

"Where did he come from?" she asked.

Leo met her concerned gaze. "It looks barely weaned. I would wager he belongs to the kitchen cat. Let us return him."

She nodded, then rose to her feet. "May I?" She held her hands to take the furry bundle.

He handed her the kitten, then scratched its head before pivoting toward the house.

His wife spent the remainder of the walk cooing to the animal. When they reached the kitchen garden, he spotted a scullery maid picking herbs. "You there."

The maid looked up, then dipped into a curtsy. "My lord."

"We found this kitten stuck in a garden bush. I imagine it belongs to the kitchen cat. See it cared for."

The maid nodded, then came forward.

"He had a thorn in his paw. We must clean the wound," Lady Morton said.

"I'll see to it at once, my lady." The servant reached for the kitten.

Before she could take the furry bundle, Lady Morton turned away, moving it out of her reach. Her gaze went to Leo's.

Lord, she was beautiful. Not in the traditional way, but stunning nonetheless. How had he missed it?

Releasing a breath, he pushed the thought from his mind. Holding her gaze, he asked, "Is there a problem?"

His wife shook her head. "No. Well..." She nibbled her lower lip. "I would like to care for Puff myself."

"Puff?" Leo asked.

She nodded. "Yes, I named him Puff, and I want to see to his needs myself."

He could not help but grin as he studied her. The protective way she now held the kitten, and the fact that she had so quickly named the creature, put a crack in his carefully crafted shield. It would seem his wife possessed a tender nature.

He glanced at the kitten, then back to Lady Morton. "Very well. If it pleases you to do so, you may."

She smiled. "I will see you at dinner."

"Until then," Leo said. He turned and walked away, reluctant to admit that he was indeed looking forward to dining with her.

CHAPTER 5

EMELINE SAT AT the far end of the dining table. She watched her husband across the vast divide as footman brought in the third course.

The space between them bothered her. She understood that they each had their place at, but it seemed ridiculous to sit so far apart, given that only the two of them were dining.

They could not talk to one another without raising their voices. Doing so would be most unbecoming, and thus, she had remained silent. But she wanted to share a conversation with him. That was the point of her insisting that they dine together.

Determination fortified her as she pinned him with her gaze. Emeline pushed out her chair and stood. She'd not allow society's dictates to keep her from her goal.

From the opposite end of the table, her husband stood, too. "What are you doing?"

She strolled around the end of the table. "I am coming to sit beside you."

"The countess sits at the foot of the table. That's the way it's done," he argued.

"Rubbish." She waved a dismissive hand. "It is not as if we are hosting guests." She stopped at the chair to the left of him, then nodded to a footman.

The servant came forward and pulled out her chosen chair.

Emeline sat, then smiled up at her husband, hoping to appear innocent. "There now. This is exceedingly better."

He stared at her for a moment, then shook his head and retook his chair.

She breathed a sigh of relief, glad that he would not argue with her further. "We could scarcely talk the way we were, and I very much wish to talk, my lord."

He tipped his wineglass and drank. After setting it back on the table, he lifted his fork.

Evidently, he would not volunteer a topic. Still, Emeline would not be dissuaded. She stared at him until he met her gaze, then asked, "What shall I call you? 'My lord' hardly seems right, considering that you are my husband now. Surely we needn't be so formal."

"Morton will suit," he said.

She shook her head. "Not in the least. We are married now. Wives do not call their husbands by a title."

In truth, she wasn't sure. Mother had called her father by his first name, and so, Emeline assumed that was the proper way of things. Perhaps she was wrong, but even so, she did not want to be so formal with the earl.

Frown lines creased the side of his mouth as he stared at her. The light of flickering candles reflected in his eyes, along with the flicker of something else. Some emotions she could not name. "Very well, then. You can call me Quinton."

Quinton. She pondered the name. It could be his first name, but she would wager it to be his surname or that of another title he held. She sighed. "I would rather use your given name. I know the day will come when our son wishes to know it. Imagine how foolish I would look having to admit that I do not know my own husband's name."

He swallowed a bite of mutton. "Don't you think it too intimate to address each other so informally?"

"Too intimate?" she repeated, half in question and half in disbelief. "I am your wife. Your countess. You plan to bed me this very night. I hardly think calling each other by name is more intimate than all that." She took a fortifying gulp of her wine. "Your name, if you please." This time, she more demanded than asked.

He blew out a breath, returning his gaze to her. "If you insist, you may call me Leonard, but only when we are alone."

"It is my wish to do so, Leonard." she tried the name out and found that she liked the way it rolled from her tongue, though it was a bit cumbersome. Perhaps she would call him Leo instead.

Would he object?

Maybe it would be best if she stuck to Leonard for now. She smiled. "It is an excellent name. Strong and bold like the man who carries it."

He attempted to hide his grin behind his napkin, but she saw it despite his effort. At that moment, she likened him to a wounded beast. Not entirely unlike her new kitten, though, it would seem Leonard was more guarded.

She could not help but wonder why. Nor could she fight the rising urge to discover his reasons.

She would tame him. She'd made her mind up to do as much the moment she'd wed him. Her conviction had only grown in the hours since. His hesitance to answer her questions in the garden had piqued her curiosity. She wanted to learn his secrets. But this man possessed more than secrets. His tenderness with Puff had softened her heart. She suspected he was a man capable of great love.

Perhaps she was a fool, but she very much hoped to convert this marriage of convenience into one of tender regard.

She sat her wine down and searched out his attention. "And you will call me Emeline. No Lady Morton or ma'am."

His eyes narrowed.

Her hand stilled, her fork hovering halfway between her plate and mouth. "It is nothing more than a name. No harm will come from using it."

He nodded, then asked, "How does the kitten fare?"

"Puff is well. I put a salve on his paw and gave him some warm milk. He's been sleeping in a basket since. The poor dear. He's worn out from his ordeal."

"I have every confidence he is in excellent hands," Leonard said before turning his attention back to his meal.

Emeline's cheeks warmed at the compliment. It would seem that her husband held a high opinion of her—leastwise when it came to tending injured animals.

Regardless, she would consider it a splendid start in earning his admiration.

She finished her mutton in silence, stealing glances at him now and again.

When the footmen began clearing the course, she turned to him again. "I have a surprise for you."

His eyebrows arched, causing his forehead to wrinkle. "I would rather you not bother yourself—"

"There is no need to protest. It cost me nothing more than time. It is but a small thing, you'll see. A trifle truly." She looked at the footman across from her and nodded.

A footman carried in a silver tray and set it before them on the table.

Emeline glanced from the crystal bowls laden with lemon cream to her husband. "I made it myself. A small gesture meant to bring you a smile."

His jaw slackened, and his eyes widened, showing his genuine surprise. "No one has ever..." his voice trailed off as he looked back at the creamy dish. "That is…"

"I enjoyed every moment." She beamed at him as she lifted one of the bowls and held it out. "Do have some."

CHAPTER 6

L EO COULD SCARCELY help but be in awe over his wife's gesture. Not only had the woman listened to what he'd said previously, but acted upon it.

And it was not just the lemon cream. Oh, no. He had to stay strong in the face of her sultry looks, warm smiles, and tender actions.

How could he keep his guard up in the face of such temptation?

He feared he could not.

His only defense would be to get her with child as quickly as possible. Once her belly was swelling, she would move into another of their homes, and he would be safe.

To that end, he downed the scotch in his tumbler, then quit the library.

He strode through the house with long confident steps, his determination mounting more with each fall of his boots. By the time he reached her chamber, he was more than ready to bed her.

He wasted no time knocking, but instead pushed her door wide and stepped inside.

Leo had every intention of taking her directly to the bed and stripping her bare. He'd not expected, never even considered, he'd find her laid out on the bed waiting for him.

She smiled, slow and sultry, her brown eyes warm with invitation.

She stretched out one of her legs, exposing more skin. "Good evening, Leonard."

Her tone sent a shiver of passion straight to his groin. He reached the bed in three strides and sat on the mattress, bringing his hand to her ankle. "Good evening."

She arched a brow and pursed her lips.

"Emeline," he added as he skimmed his hand up her calf. Her flesh was warm and silken. He bent and trailed a line of kisses up the inside of her leg.

Bloody hell, his wife was luscious. Her silken skin and scandalous invitation drove him wild with desire.

She released a breathy sigh as he moved his hand up her thigh, drawing her nightrail further up her body.

He met her alluring gaze as he drew small circles on her exposed thigh. "You surprise me, wife."

Rather than speak, she reached out and took hold of his cravat. "I believe you are overdressed." She sat up, her fingers working on loosening the knot at his throat. "Allow me to help."

Leo moved his fingers closer to the apex of her thighs as she unwound his cravat.

When she set to work on his jacket, he brought his lips to her throat.

Breathy moans sounded as he nipped and sucked at the tender flesh.

She gathered his shirt in her hands and pulled it from his breeches, her warm hands delving beneath the fabric to fan across his abdomen and chest.

Leo's blood ignited, and his cock throbbed.

Bloody hell, how did she affect him so severely? If he did not take her soon, he would spill in his breeches like an inexperienced youth.

He pulled away, then stood. He removed his shirt before he unbuttoned the fall of his breeches.

Her eyes widened, then filled with desire as his cock sprang free. He stood there, allowing her to drink in the sight of him while he allowed himself a moment to gain some much-needed control.

Emeline removed her nightrail. Her gaze burned into his. "Fair is fair."

"Fair indeed," he more growled than spoke the words as he dove back into the bed.

He fastened his mouth over her rosy nipple, suckling as he moved his hand between her legs.

She tangled her fingers in his hair and moaned and arched beneath him.

His fingers found her curls and stroked through them to the core of her need. She was hot and wet for him. Her state of arousal pleased him greatly.

He wanted to plunge into her, to fill and stretch her. To claim her and satisfy his own need, but she was a virgin, and he'd not hurt her if he could avoid it.

He moved his mouth to her other nipple and stroked his finger over her moist folds. When her thighs fell open, he slipped his finger into the inviting heat.

"Oh. Ah…" She rocked against his hand. "More. I need…more."

Her breathy sighs and pleading words made him desperate to taste her. Leo brought his mouth to the tiny pearl above her opening and suckled. The scent of her drove him to near madness.

"That's the way, pet. Take what you need. Let yourself go," he encouraged as he slid a second finger into her tight passage.

He stared at her as he pumped his fingers.

She pressed her head back against the pillows, her lips slightly parted as she cried with pleasure. A cascade of gold-streaked chestnut hair fanned out around her, and her smooth skin flushed pink with desire.

She was stunning. And all his.

Leo brought his tongue to the tiny bud and licked her essence as she bucked against him. Once, twice, three laps of his tongue, then he suckled as he stroked his fingers inside of her.

"Oh. Oh, Leo." She pressed against him as she came undone. Her release washed over his fingers.

"Yes, pet?"

"That," she drew in a breath, "was nice."

"Nice?" He arched a brow.

She nodded. "Yes. Nice."

He smirked as he positioned himself between her thighs. "Then I fear I did it wrong."

"No." She shook her head. "It was... I liked what you did."

He stared into her smoldering eyes. "I shall endeavor to make you like the act of joining, too. There will be some pain, but I will do all I can to limit it. Please know that it is not my wish to hurt you."

She nibbled her lower lip, then said, "I trust you." She wrapped her legs around his hips. "And I want you deep inside of me."

Devil take it, she was a temptress. So wanton and sweet. He positioned his cock at her entrance, then pushed in, slow and steady.

When she cringed, he paused, his arms shaking with the effort to remain still.

A heartbeat later, she brought her hands to his shoulders and arched, taking him deeper. Her gaze bore into his as she said, "I want this. I want to feel you."

It was all the encouragement he needed. Leo pressed fully into her, filling her completely. This...his wife...being inside of her...was heaven.

He kissed at the flesh of her throat as he pulled out, then slid back into her. Slow, steady thrusts that pushed him closer to the edge.

"Oh, Leo."

Her moans filled the chamber once more. She moved with him, her hips following his rhythm. Her cunny pulsed with release as he plowed into her again and again.

His orgasm tore through him, and his seed pumped into her.

After allowing himself a minute to recover, he slid his cock free and moved to sit on the edge of the bed.

She reached out and feathered her hand down his back.

Lord, how he wanted to gather her close and hold her through the night. Instead, he stood and retrieved his clothing from the floor.

When he turned to look at her, his heart hitched.

She stared back at him, her gaze full of tenderness. "Won't you stay?" She licked her lips. "At least for a while?"

He swallowed back a groan. "I cannot."

She pushed up on her elbows. "You cannot, or you will not?"

"Both," Leo said, then turned toward the door. "I'll have a bath brought up."

He could feel her gaze on him as he exited the room, but she did not speak.

A small blessing to be sure, for she'd already said too much.

Bloody hell, she'd said she trusted him!

What's more, her actions proved that she did. Emeline had opened herself to him without reserve. She'd given herself to him without objection, without maidenly fear.

She'd seduced him as much as he had her.

Maybe more so.

She had been sweet and soft and inviting. She'd called him Leo. Not Leonard, but Leo.

The woman had driven him mad with desire, then left him more satisfied than he could ever recall being before.

And she trusted him.

Devil take it, another fracture formed in the armor surrounding his heart.

CHAPTER 7

E MELINE SLID INTO the copper tub. Warm water wrapped around her and seeped into her sore muscles. She tipped her head back and closed her eyes, a barrage of feelings and thoughts swirling through her.

Lovemaking had been marvelous.

The pain she'd worried about hadn't been so bad, it was more of a discomfort truly, and it had passed quickly, leaving pure bliss in its wake.

Even now, her body bore the afterglow. She felt somehow lighter and a bit tingly. Her limbs were like pudding, and her heart joyous.

She could get used to sharing her bed with Leo. It would be easy to welcome her husband, easier still to fall in love with him.

Emeline hummed as she splashed warm, jasmine-scented water over her chest. He had been gentle and attentive and wicked in the most delectable ways.

But then he'd left.

A frown pulled at her lips.

She was no stranger to the feeling of abandonment, nor did she like it. Leo's disregard put her in mind of *him*—the rogue from her past. Only this was not at all the same. Leo married her, where the rogue walked away.

She would not allow past hurts to weigh her down now. She had forgiven herself as well as the rogue. Emeline had moved on with her life. Still...

After what she and Leo had shared, it seemed wrong for him to make a hasty retreat. Shouldn't they snuggle and talk? At the very least, shouldn't they sleep side by side?

She may have been a virgin, but she was far from uneducated. She knew what happened when a man and a woman joined. She understood the biology of the act. And she knew lovers often shared more than their bodies.

What held Leo back? Why was he so disconnected? So guarded?

He hadn't even kissed her—not on the lips.

Her skin flushed at the thought of all the places he had kissed. Her legs, her hip, her breasts... But not her lips. Why?

"I've come to wash your hair, my lady."

Emeline opened her eyes and turned toward the maid that had entered. A sturdy, youthful woman with kind grey eyes and honey-colored hair.

If Emeline had to guess, she would say the maid must be in her late twenties.

She straightened to sit up in the tub and returned the maid's smile. "Thank you."

The servant soaped up her hands, then reached for Emeline's hair. "Lord Morton assigned me as your lady's maid. My name is Anna, and I am pleased to serve you. I do hope you find me to your liking, my lady."

"I am certain we will get on well, Anna." Emeline wrapped her arms around her legs and rested her chin on her knees. "How long have you served the earl?"

"Only since his return. Before that, I served as the late countess's maid."

Late countess? Had Leo been married before? Or did she refer to his mother? It was striking how little Emeline knew about her husband. She tipped her head back so Anna could rinse the soap and asked, "Returned from where?"

"The war, of course." Anna poured a pitcher of warm water over her hair. "The late earl bought him a commission for his twentieth birthday. 'Course, no one expected him to be called up. The late countess was beside herself with worry when it happened. After that, everything changed."

So, Leo had been a soldier.

Emeline turned the information over in her mind.

His father had purchased a commission for him, and he'd gone to war.

Leo must have been the spare. *Debrit's* would have told her as much. Perhaps she should see if there was a copy in the library. She might still learn something from looking his family up. There were so many questions to be answered.

What happened to his brother, then? Was the late countess his brother's wife? No, it must have been his mother. What happened to her? To all of them?

"I cannot imagine that he expected things to turn out as they have either," Anna continued. "It must have been quite a shock to come home and find that he was now the earl."

Emeline stood, then stepped from the tub. As Anna wrapped her in a towel, Emeline asked, "What happened to his family?"

"You don't know?" Anna arched a brow. "I thought everyone knew about the tragedy. It's just that no one speaks of it." She took a towel to Emeline's hair, rubbing the moisture from it.

Emeline's heart seemed to pause as she waited for the maid to speak again.

This woman had the answers she sought. Emeline was sure of it.

And unlike *Debrit's*, Anna stood before her.

"But never mind that. I will tell you." Anna held out her dressing gown. "They were all killed in a carriage accident. Lord and Lady Morton, along with Lord Granger and his pregnant wife. All of them gone in the blink of an eye. And only a week before the new Lord Morton returned."

Heavens! No wonder Leo did not wish to talk about his family. He must suffer unspeakable pain. Emeline could not imagine losing her entire family at one time. The loss of her father had left her bereft. Heartbroken and hollow for the longest time. Even now, she missed him dearly, but at least she still had Mother.

Leo had no one.

The war. It had only recently ended. "How long has Lord Morton been home?" She held her breath as Anna pulled a brush through her hair.

"Two weeks, my lady."

Good heavens! His wound was fresh. And yet, she saw no signs of mourning.

Leo wore a black jacket, but most men did. Absent were black gloves or bands. Neither did the servants wear mourning clothes. How strange.

Perhaps his grief was so crushing that he preferred to be in a state of denial? Maybe he found it more comfortable to ignore the tragedy and press forward than to acknowledge it.

And to think, he bore the scars of war, too.

She could not imagine what he had been through. Her heart ached for him.

"They were all laid to rest in the family cemetery mere days before he returned," Anna said as she twisted Emeline's hair into a long braid. "Lord Morton refused to visit the graves and ordered everyone to carry on as normal."

"The poor man."

"Indeed." Anna stepped back, then moved to stand in front of Emeline. "Will you be needing anything else this evening?"

"No." She shook her head. "No, thank you." And she meant the words with sincerity. Anna had been exceedingly forthcoming. Thanks to her, she now had a far greater understanding of her husband.

The door clicked shut, and Emeline sighed. No wonder Leo seemed so guarded. Grief held him in its tight fist. More than anything, he needed love and comfort.

Puff dropped a balled-up piece of parchment near her foot, then batted one paw at her bare toes, then meowed.

She scooped the kitten up, bringing it to rest on her lap. "There, there, darling. No need to fuss." She stroked the kitten's fur as she considered everything Anna had told her. No doubt remained that Leo needed someone, and she wanted to be that person. The one to comfort and care for him. The person to help him heal. But how could she use what she had learned to his benefit?

She wasn't sure, but one thing was certain, she was determined not to fail him.

CHAPTER 8

R IVULETS OF RAIN slid down the parlor window against a backdrop of grey sky and soggy landscape.

Leo had hoped to take Emeline for their usual walk outside this afternoon, but the weather forced him to keep her indoors. In an effort to maintain a distance, as well as to keep her occupied, he had a deck of cards laid out.

Thus far, his plan was working. Her attention remained on the game at hand rather than him. He had caught her casting the occasional glance his way, but she'd refrained from delving into his life with her usual barrage of questions.

"Ninety-two," Emeline said as she scooped up the trick.

Leo dealt the next hand without comment. He looked at Emeline for a heartbeat before turning to his cards.

She wore a marked look of concentration, and he wondered if she possessed the skill to count cards?

The way she was winning made him suspect she must.

He glanced out the rain-splattered window again, then back to his cards. She would likely take this trick as well, for his hand was rubbish. Not that he cared. In truth, he enjoyed watching her play so expertly.

She'd had already won two games, and considering she had a twenty-three-point lead, she would claim victory again.

"Carte blanche." Emeline laid her cards out face up for Leo to see. "And that makes one hundred and two. I win." She smiled.

"Congratulations on a game well played." He scooped up the cards, then handed her the deck. "Your deal."

She scowled at the offering. "I am weary of cards. Do let us promenade around the parlor." She turned her smile on him. "I would very much enjoy the opportunity to stretch my limbs."

Leo wanted to deny her, but the gentleman in him would not allow it. He had agreed to spend an hour with her, and so he must.

Reluctantly, he nodded, then stood to offer her his arm. A tendril of heat unfurled, traveling up his arm at her touch.

"Are you not the least bit curious why I agreed to marry you?" she asked.

It seemed today's inquisition would focus on her.

He released a pent-up breath. Better to discuss her than him, though there was still a danger in it.

He did not wish to get close, and the more they grew to know one another, the harder it would be to guard himself.

Bloody hell, the woman already had him lusting after her to the point of distraction. He'd lain awake for hours last night, fighting the urge to return to her bed, and woke up hard as a rock this morning with her on his mind.

"Well?" She slid her glance his way. One eyebrow arched in question.

"You needed money."

"And you don't wonder why that was?"

He led her along the back of the parlor, their footfalls tapping out a slow rhythm against the polished floor. "It doesn't signify."

"But of course it does. For all you know, I am some sort of criminal. A thief, perhaps."

Amusement piqued Leo's interest as he met her gaze, a teasing grin playing at his lips. "Shall I instruct the housekeeper to guard the silver?"

"That won't be necessary."

"Perhaps I should call Bow Street, then?" He did his best to appear serious. "Or have our union annulled."

She swatted at him, her small hand giving a light whack to his bicep. "Hush now. You'd see us both as social pariahs."

He feigned seriousness as he stared at her. "It seems my hands are tied. I can either await my murder or see us to ruin."

"I'm a murderer now?" she asked, her eyes sparkling.

"You are the one who told me you might be dangerous. Are you not?"

She grinned with mischief. "That I did, however, I only meant to pique your interest."

"And so you have. Now tell me what led you to such desperation."

Leo's present enjoyment was so great that he forgot his reluctance as genuine curiosity tickled him. This woman, his wife, proved to be a marvelous distraction from his brooding.

"Very well," she averted her gaze back to the path in front of them. "You already know my father was a physician. What you do not know is that he was quite successful. He kept Mother and me in the latest fashions, our home was grand by most standards, and we never wanted for food. He was frugal to a point but never denied us anything. I had a dowry, and when he passed away, his account held enough coin to see Mother and me through."

Leo noted the fine lines creasing her brow. The little flecks in her deep brown eyes seemed to fade as she inhaled a slow breath. He patted her hand where it rested on his elbow. "You need not continue if you do not wish to."

"Please. I want you to understand."

Leo nodded, then led her around the corner of the parlor to stroll toward the fireplace.

"I grew up in a loving and secure home. When Father died, it shattered me. Mother and I wept for weeks. Months even before we resumed any sort of regularity. When we emerged from mourning, Mother comforted and distracted us with lavish trips and shopping expeditions."

Emeline stilled and turned to Leo.

"She was so used to having money and to Father keeping the accounts healthy that she never considered where we would get more. Not until the creditors came, and she lacked the funds they required. That is when my dowry disappeared, and we were suddenly impoverished."

His heart squeezed as he studied her. A sheen of unshed tears clouded her eyes, and her lips quivered.

How the devil was he to remain aloft when her every word and action beckoned him near?

He wanted to comfort her, but he also wanted to run from her. She wasn't supposed to require more than money from him, and now, here she stood in need of comfort.

His fingers twitched as his heart ached, but he held still.

Bloody hell, he wanted to make her feel better, but he could not cross that line.

"I should have known better, too. It is not all Mother's fault. Even if it were, as her daughter, I bore a responsibility to marry. The job of saving us fell to me, and so I married you." A rogue tear slipped from her eye.

Leo could no longer ignore her plight. He reached out and dashed the offending teardrop from her cheek. "Don't fret. I am not all that bad. You are a countess now, and I already promised to care for you and your mother. All will be well. You have my word."

Emeline pressed her eyes closed and nodded. Her thick, dark lashes fluttered, her gaze seeking his. "And I have promised you an heir. I confess to being curious as to why you were in such a hurry as to marry a stranger."

Bloody hell, he should have known she'd turn the topic back to him. A turn for a turn, or some such other rubbish. He scrubbed a hand over his jaw. He supposed he could give her a crumb. Just enough to satisfy her. "I have a responsibility to my tenants and title."

"Indeed," she drawled, "but you are handsome and titled, you could have your pick of women. Why choose a stranger? Why rush to the altar?"

Instead of answering, he tugged her into his arms, crushing his mouth against hers.

CHAPTER 9

EMELINE CLUNG TO Leo as his mouth devoured hers in a bruising kiss. He demanded more, and she parted her lips, allowing his tongue to dart inside her mouth.

Her knees weakened as she brought her arms around his neck. Passion swam through her, threatening to choke off all reason.

This kiss had little to do with passion. It was little more than an attempt to quiet her. He had no wish to answer her questions. No wish to discuss his past, but it was too important to ignore.

She fought the urge to get lost in the moment and pulled back.

Her breaths came fast as she splayed her hand on his chest, holding him at bay. "That was some kiss, and I would like to do it more, but not right now." She gave a weak smile, her heart pounding. "Presently, I wish to talk."

"You talk too much," he half growled as he leaned toward her again.

She took a step back. "On the contrary, you do not talk enough."

"We do not need to talk at all."

Emeline stiffened and notched her chin. "I understand your reluctance to discuss your family, can you not understand my desire to know you?"

Leo stared at her, his eyes holding no expression. "You agreed to give me a son. Friendship was not a part of the bargain."

"I think you are worth knowing. Worth caring about and building a life with."

"Then you are mistaken." His tone was frosty.

Emeline fought the urge to pull back. "I will be the judge of that."

He placed his hand over hers where it rested on his cheek and held it in place. His other arm snaked around her waist and pulled her tight against him.

Desire sparked, and her pulse thrummed at the feel of his muscled torso tight against her body. It would be all too easy to press her lips to his.

The temptation to allow his distraction mounted when she took account of her situation.

Her breasts were molded to his chest, his erection pressed to her abdomen, and heat pooled between her thighs. To her dismay, a small whimper escaped her lips.

"I want you, now," he whispered close to her ear.

"I want to know why you did not tell me you were a soldier?"

His hold on her faltered. "It is irrelevant."

She stroked her hand over his jawline. "It makes you a hero."

He shook his head. "I'm no hero. I am scared, inside. Cold and empty." He met her gaze and stared deep into her eyes. "Do yourself a favor and cease your efforts to make more of us than we are."

"Never," she said with conviction. She had taken him to husband and would not abandon him now. This was her life, her future. She'd not give up on them. "I want a—"

His mouth claimed hers once more, cutting off her words.

This time, Emeline succumbed. She trailed her hand from his jaw into his hair and wrapped her arm around his neck.

Perhaps, for now, she could comfort him without words. Mayhap, she could take a bit for herself, too.

He trailed kisses across to her ear and whispered, "I need to be inside you."

"Yes."

He spun her around, then pulled her back against him. His lips found the side of her neck as his hand slid up her belly to cup her breast.

Her skin tingled as her need grew. Her core pulsed, and dampness pooled between her legs. She tried to turn back to face him, to demand he take her this instant, but he stilled her.

"Stay. I want you like this." He reached for her skirt and tugged it up to her waist. "Say you want me, too. Say you trust me."

"I want you." She pressed her backside tight against him and wriggled. "I trust you."

His hand slipped around to cup her mound, and liquid fire pooled in her core.

A moan ripped from her throat when he slid his finger into her heat.

She bent forward, her pleasure building. "Leo, now. I need you now," she begged as she ground against him.

He kissed the back of her neck as he fumbled with his breeches. A moment later, his manhood caressed her backside, telling her he was more than ready to take her.

On instinct, she spread her thighs farther and arched her back. "Leo... please." She sighed as he slid into her.

"Put your hands on the back of the couch," he ordered as he pulled out, then thrust back into her heat.

Emeline did as told, stretching her arms out and taking hold of the brocade cloth.

The movement brought him deeper into her, and she bucked back, wanting even more.

The man's touch rendered her a complete wanton, and she didn't bother to hide it. She loved every moment of their coupling. Every wicked touch, every scorching kiss, and every thrust.

"Yes," she cried as he took hold of her hips and thrust harder, deeper.

She could quickly become addicted to this. To him. Perhaps she already was. She turned her head as far as she could manage, her gaze meeting his.

"Come for me, pet. Come now," he said.

As if she had no choice, she cried out in bliss.

His cock pulsed within her as a rush of warmth filled her.

She whimpered when he pulled out of her and turned to embrace him.

He wrapped his arms around her, his heart beating against her ear. He smoothed his hand over her hair, down her back. "Go clean up, pet," he said, then released her and strode toward the parlor door.

She bit back a protest as she watched him go.

More than anything, she wanted to stay in his arms.

Why did he always run off afterword? And why the devil didn't he kiss her while they made love? She'd thought it odd the first time, but now? Now it seemed to be a pattern.

But then, he had kissed her soundly beforehand.

Perhaps she was making too much of it. After all, how does one kiss a person who has their back to them?

She blushed at the wickedness of their joining and wondered at the pleasure she found in his arms.

If he experienced one fraction of what she felt, he would never let her go.

Lord knew she couldn't walk away from him.

Not now.

Not ever.

Certainly not of her own choice.

Somehow, some way, she had to win his heart. This marriage of convenience had turned into something much more profound for her. She cared for him. Emeline wanted to build a life with him.

CHAPTER 10

CANDLELIGHT FLICKERED FROM the center of the table, casting Emeline in a soft glow. Leo studied her as he sipped his wine. She'd taken him by surprise this afternoon—first with her knowledge of his military service and then with her unbridled passion. He could scarcely help but wonder what other surprises she had in store.

His heart tugged when the corner of her mouth pulled down. She turned shadowed eyes on him, and he swallowed hard.

Had he upset her in some way?

Setting his wineglass down, he asked, "Is something troubling you?"

She sighed. "It is only that I do not have much of an appetite this evening."

Neither did he. Not for food, at any rate. His tempting imp of a wife was another thing, altogether. He was half-starved for her, despite their afternoon tryst.

How beastly of him to think about plundering her at this moment—over the dinner table and while she seemed so out of sorts. Still, he could not help but entertain the thought of laying her down and plunging deep into her heat.

His cock lacked manners, too, for it now tented his breeches.

Leo pressed his eyes closed and drew in a slow breath. This was not the time for sexual deviance. He opened his eyes and met her stare. "Is the food not to your liking? I can have cook send something else up."

"That isn't it at all." She shook her head.

"Are you ill? Shall I send for the doctor?"

She shook her head again. "I'm quite well. Thank you."

"Then what is it?" he asked, confusion dousing his ardor. "Did you have a large afternoon meal or a late snack?"

Emeline smiled. "Only if you count." Her cheeks turned rose-colored as she added, "As a snack, that is."

Wicked images sprang back to life in his mind.

More than anything, he wanted to be inside her, thrusting deep.

He needed to possess her. To make her as wild as she made him.

He gave a teasing wink. "I do believe that qualifies."

"Good." She leaned closer across the table. "In that case, I want dessert."

He quirked a brow. "You surprise me, wife."

Her cheeks flamed, but she held his gaze. "The more often we join, the faster I will conceive."

"Very true," he agreed.

"I want you again. I want you often." Her tongue darted out to lick her lower lip. "I want you now."

He'd never heard anything more erotic. Her words rendered him powerless. He could no more deny her than he could stop the sun from setting.

Leo slid his chair back and stood. It one smooth move he was at her side.

She gave a slight squeal of delight as he lifted her into his arms. Her hands snaked around his shoulders, and she nuzzled her face against his neck.

Desire shot through him with such force it stole his breath.

She gave a teasing nip, her teeth pulling at his cravat. "Hurry," she demanded.

He carried her from the room with long strides, then took the stairs two at a time. The urge to resist and guard himself, all but crumbled in the face of her seduction. All at once, he could imagine a life with her. A real union filled with sexual delight, friendship, and shared burdens.

He pushed back against the thoughts as he laid her on the over-stuffed mattress and came down beside her.

Emeline kissed his jaw, his forehead, his lips…

Leo studied her while she worked to remove his cravat, then turned her attention to his jacket and waistcoat.

"I want to love you," she said as she pulled his shirt free of his breeches.

Love. The word curled around his heart like an iron fist. He well knew where that particular emotion led.

Could he risk it again? Could he relax and trust her? Devil take it, he wanted to.

She brought her lips to his abdomen and licked and suckled his burning flesh as she continued to lift his shirt. "Let me love you," she said, her breath hot against his skin.

Need coiled so tight within him, he found himself powerless to do anything other than concede to her wishes.

Leo nodded, then pulled his shirt over his head. His pulse raced as she pushed him back on the bed.

She straddled him, then wriggled as she worked to remove her gown.

How did this tiny woman affect him in such a powerful way?

Leo needed to take back some semblance of control. He reached out and grabbed her waist, stilling her. "Let me help."

Her gaze burned into his as he reached behind her to loosen her fastenings. Buttons. He nearly groaned. There must be hundreds of tiny, well-secured buttons holding the gown shut. Having no patience for them, Leo grabbed both sides of the gown and pulled it apart.

She did not seem to care as she shimmied out of the dress, letting it pool at her waist, then slipping it off completely.

She leaned forward, lowering her breasts toward his face, and he captured one nipple. She moaned and wiggled as he suckled and teased. First one, then the other.

Releasing her breast, he met her warm gaze full of tenderness and heat. "I want to be inside of you."

"I want that, too," she said.

He reached for her, intent to flip her on her back.

She swatted at his hands and scooted down his body until her bottom was seated near his knees.

He watched in shock and awe as she reached for his falls.

When his cock sprang free, she did the most unexpected thing.

The little minx kissed the tip of his erection.

She ran her tongue down the length of him, then flicked it across the tip. "You like that. I can see that you do."

She required no answer. She lowered her head and took him in her mouth.

Fervent need burned through him as he fought against the urge to wrap his fingers in her hair and thrust into her sweet, inviting mouth.

"Stop," he ordered through clenched teeth.

She glanced up at him, her eyes wide. "Did I hurt you?"

"No. It… You feel too damn good."

"Then, why stop?" She gave a saucy grin.

"Another moment of that, and I'll spill my seed. I do not wish to rob you of your pleasure."

"Oh," she said, reaching between them to stroke his abdomen. "Tell me what you want."

His wife was an angel, and he was quickly coming to realize he didn't deserve her.

Regardless, he had her. She was his wife, today, tomorrow, and always. Perhaps he could make an effort to trust her.

This demonstration of hers proved that she trusted him. Perhaps it would not be so foolish to open his heart after all.

But then, he wasn't sure he even had a heart left to open—not a functional one worthy of her.

"How do I make love to you? Tell me what to do?"

He groaned with need before finding his tongue to reply. "Straddle me and take your pleasure."

He saw a moment's hesitation, then she lowered herself, taking his cock deep inside.

She rocked, slowly at first, then faster as she found her rhythm.

She felt so damn good, and he wondered if he would ever get enough.

Leo tangled his fingers in her long, glossy hair and pulled her mouth to his.

He kissed her deeply, soundly, drinking her in.

He'd lost control, and it felt good.

Damn good.

CHAPTER 11

B ODY SATED, EMELINE collapsed atop Leo, resting her head on his chest. Their hearts pounded together as she swirled her fingertips over his dampened skin.

She'd never been so satisfied. So happy.

He stroked his hand over her head. "I lost control."

Control of what? She wondered at his statement and how, or even if she should reply.

In the end, she settled for, "I'm glad you did." Because whatever he was on about, she'd enjoyed it and wanted more.

Leo rolled her off of him, then started to get up.

Emeline wrapped her arm around his waist. "Stay." She found his gaze and stared into his grey eyes. "Hold me, at least until I fall asleep."

She felt his muscles tighten beneath her touch and saw the look of indecision. Did he find her too repulsive to stay? She didn't think so, for if he did, she doubted he would bed her with such vigor.

No, there was something else behind his desire to flee. But what?

"You don't have to cuddle with me, but stay for a while."

He relaxed against the pillows and drew her into his embrace. "Just until you fall asleep."

"Thank you," she said, snuggling against his warm, hard body.

She closed her eyes and attempted to sleep, but her mind would not cease its speculation. His earlier words came back to her. *I lost control.* Had he referred to the soul-shattering kiss he'd given her while they'd made love?

That would explain so much. Everything, really.

Not kissing her while they joined, the way he always left her the moment they finished, his reserved nature, and desire to spend as little time as possible in her company. It was all in an effort to guard himself.

She eased her head up, searching for his gaze. Her lips parted to speak, but she swallowed back the words.

It had been on the tip of her tongue to ask him outright if he was afraid to love her. However, she did not wish to sound accusatory. Nor did she think pushing him would be to her benefit.

Instead, she caressed his jawline, then cupped his cheek. When he turned his gaze on her, she whispered, "I could love you. If you let me."

His expression went soft. A flicker of something, hope perhaps, flashed through the depths of his eyes, then he pulled her back to his chest. "Sleep, pet," he said.

She closed her eyes again and let the steady beat of his heart lull her to sleep. When dawn broke, and she rubbed the sleep from her eyes, he was gone.

They spent the next fortnight in much the same way.

He gave Emeline an hour in the afternoon and joined her until she fell asleep at night. They made love all over the house. Sometimes he took her bent over furniture or pressed against the wall in an alcove. More than once, he had laid her out on the carpet before the fire. And every night, without fail, he brought her to raptures in her bedchamber.

He was tender and encouraged her sensuality.

Emeline found it heady and empowering to share her bed, her body. She reveled in their lovemaking and always craved more. But still, she found herself alone each morning.

As much as she relished being naked in his arms, she craved the time they spent together with their clothes on.

During the past fortnight, they had gone riding, walked through the garden, played cards, and spilikins, and ventured out into London to visit Hyde Park and Gunters.

She found his company enjoyable. He proved to be witty and protective, and his touch never failed to ignite her blood.

Leo seemed to be opening up to her in small measures. A fact that she found encouraging. And while he had yet to share anything about his family or the tragedy that befell them, he opened up about other things.

She felt them growing closer and prayed it was not her imagination for, in truth, she'd fallen irrevocably in love with the man who was as wild as a lion in her bed.

And today, she had a surprise for him.

She turned at the sound of footfalls and laid her hand on her abdomen. Giddiness swelled up in her as Leo strode toward the fountain.

Heavens, if he wasn't the most handsome man in all of England. All the world, for that matter.

He left her positively breathless.

LEO'S STEP FALTERED at the sight of Emeline lighting up for him. She almost glowed in the wash of sunlight. A faint blush covered her cheeks, and her eyes sparkled as she started toward him.

In another heartbeat, she was running toward him, her skirts held high.

He held out his arms in invitation, and she raced into them.

"I have a surprise for you," she said as she embraced him.

He hugged her close and inhaled her scent. Today she radiated honeysuckle and mint. The smell sweet and soothing, just as she was.

He smiled against her hair and said, "I gathered as much when I found your note. Tell me, minx, what mischief are you about?"

When Leo went to meet her for their afternoon in the parlor, he found a perfumed note instead of his wife. The letter merely read *'meet me by the fountain.'*

Curious as to what she was doing, he wasted no time joining her.

He released her and stepped back to peer over her shoulder at the fountain. Nothing looked out of place.

He scanned the surrounding grounds.

Again, everything looked as it should.

He turned his attention back to her. "Do you intend to keep me in suspense?"

She giggled. "A little suspense is good for you."

"Minx."

"You like it." She threaded her arm through his and urged him to walk. "I would rather show you than tell you."

He allowed her to guide him toward the massive marble and granite fountain, all the while wondering what he would discover.

Did she intend to push him into the water? He slid his gaze to her.

Judging by the mischievous grin and air of playfulness she wore, he didn't doubt that she might. "Are we to go for a swim?"

She shook her head. "Of course not."

"Then, it is only me who is meant to get wet?" He tugged her toward him, then stared into her eyes. "You intend to drown me. Is that it?"

"Only if you plan to provoke me."

He chuckled. "Is that what I'm doing?"

"You are verging on it." She released his arm. "Now close your eyes. No peeking," she ordered.

Leo peered at her, unsure whether he should obey or refuse.

"Go on. Do it." She nodded. "I promise not to do anything untoward. Trust me."

There was that word again. *Trust.* The very thing that had given him so much pain. The people who he'd trusted most in this world had all betrayed him. Now, his sweet wife wanted him to trust her. He studied her, his gaze searching deep within hers.

"Please," she begged, a bit of the playfulness fading from her eyes.

He exhaled slowly, his throat growing tight. Then he shocked himself by saying, "Very well."

She took hold of his arms. "Keep them closed, and let me guide you." She took a small step, pulling him forward.

Leo's mind protested, his instincts screamed for him to open his eyes, but he kept them firmly shut.

He had nothing to fear.

What could she possibly do to him? Out here with no one and nothing save for the shrubs and fountain.

Relax, he told himself as sweat beaded on his forehead. Even if she beat him with a tulip, he'd survive. A refreshing bath in the fountain would scarcely kill him. All would be fine.

She released her hold on him. "Keep them closed. Remember, you promised."

He nodded. The sound of her footsteps crushing the gravel path tickled his ears, then faded.

Where had she gone?

To retrieve a pistol, perhaps.

That was preposterous, and he knew it. Still, what the devil was she up to?

Surely a quick peek would hurt nothing.

She would never know he'd cheated, and doing so would calm his nerves.

He cracked one eye open, then slammed it shut at the sound of her returning.

Damn and blast! He hadn't seen a thing.

"Do you trust me?" she asked again.

He nodded. "If I did not, I wouldn't have allowed you to lead me blindly through the garden." To Leo's amazement, his words were genuine. He did trust her.

"Excellent. Hold out your hand."

He held it out, and she took hold of his wrist. Trepidation made the tiny hairs at the nape of his neck stand on end.

Now she went too far. He opened his eyes, and his heart hitched.

"You cheated!" she squealed.

"It was a reflex. I could scarcely help it." He shook his head. "For all I knew, you were about to cut my hand off."

She narrowed her eyes. "Ah... I cannot believe..."

"Come here." He reached for her and drew her close. "I'm sorry." His gaze roamed to the fishing pole she held. "What are we to do with those?"

"Fish, of course."

She said it as though it were the most natural thing in the world to go fishing in a garden without a pond or lake in sight.

"What precisely are we aiming to catch?" he asked with genuine curiosity.

"Why birds, of course." She handed him a pole, her expression serious. "Unless you would rather cast for flowers."

"Flowers it is." He tested the weight and length of the pole in his hand. She'd chosen well.

Emeline took a few steps back, then turned away from him. "I'll show you how it's done."

Surely, she didn't intend to hook a plant.

Splash.

The sinker broke the surface of the fountain's water.

Emeline glanced over her shoulder to smile at him. "No flowers in there, I'm afraid."

"But I suspect there may be something else." He strode over to the fountain and peered into the water.

His heart swelled at the sight.

Several rainbow-colored fish swam about, their scales reflecting the sun's rays. How had she managed it? More importantly, why go to so much trouble for him?

He bent to dip his fingers in the cool water. A large trout swam up and nibbled at his fingertip.

No one had ever done something like this for him. Not a single person had ever put so much thought into a surprise for him, and it warmed his heart. Hell, it warmed his soul.

"Do you like it? My surprise?"

He pivoted to face her. The way she nibbled her lower lip and stared expectantly at him arrowed straight to his heart.

No doubt about it, she was nervous. He strode toward her. "I love it."

A wide smile lit Emeline's face as he scooped her into his arms. "You do?"

"I do."

She dropped a quick kiss to his jawline. "Then what are you waiting for? Go on. Cast your line."

He chuckled as he bent to retrieve his pole. "Are we to have trout for supper?"

"Cook is expecting a fresh haul."

It would seem that his wife thought of everything. He'd told her he enjoyed fishing, and she'd not only taken note but figured out a way for them to do so right here in their garden.

He should not be so taken aback. She had a way of doing little things that endeared her to him. It had started with the lemon cream, and there had been so many things since.

The tenderness in her touch, the way she trusted him with her body and welfare, the way she spoke so freely of her past and welcomed him into her life. He found himself wanting to hold her and protect her.

If he were honest, he'd admit that she had already thawed his frozen heart. He'd come to cherish her and the time they spent together.

More than once, he'd completely forgotten the pain of his past. A few times, he had dared to want more time with her, more feelings to develop between them. Perhaps he should reach for her and what she offered.

Maybe, just maybe, she was different. Hadn't she already proven as much?

She could have married him, accepted his nightly visits, and ignored him the rest of the time. Instead, she demanded he spend time with her. She went out of her way to make him smile and listened when he spoke.

But he'd been terribly wrong before. Lucinda's pretty face and words had blinded Leo. She'd declared her love, and he'd fallen right into her trap. He could not allow himself to be used like that again.

Somewhere inside, he knew Emeline was different. Her actions spoke volumes.

She cared for him, but could she love him?

Her words from before drifted through his mind, *'I could love you. If you let me'*.

Could Leo trust her? More importantly, did he want her to love him?

At this point, did he even have a choice?

CHAPTER 12

E MELINE SUSPECTED SHE was with child when her courses failed to arrive on time. She remained silent because she did not want to give false hope, but also because she did not want to part with Leo.

She hadn't had enough time with him, maybe she never would. Nonetheless, she needed more for him to fall in love with her.

These past weeks had convinced her he was well on his way. She still found herself alone each morning, but he no longer pushed her away.

They had taken to spending much of the day together, rather than the hour she had negotiated for. And sometimes when he didn't think she was paying attention, Emeline caught him watching her with a tenderness in his gaze.

Surely it meant something. If not love, then at least a deep affection.

She prayed she was right. For now, she knew without a doubt that she was expecting. She hadn't had courses since before they married. Her appetite had changed, and she spent the previous three mornings hunched over her chamber pot, casting up her accounts.

Her heart would break if he turned away from her now.

Not only because she loved him, but because she knew he could love her. More than anything, she wanted them to be a family.

The rogue had taught Emeline how cruel men could be. He had deceived her. Made her believe he wanted to marry her, that he loved her. In the end, after she refused to lift her skirts, he'd left her. It took her years to forgive herself, and more to forgive him.

This was different. Leo was her husband. He had married her.

She exhaled a slow breath as she stared out the drawing room window.

Emeline turned her attention to Leo. He sat in a high-back chair near the hearth with his long, muscular legs stretched out and crossed at the ankles. The two of them had taken to spending their evenings this way. Relaxing together.

Tonight, however, was different. Her nerves were on edge as she fretted over how he would react to her news. She wasn't sure how to tell him. Should she simply state the fact? Or should she tease a bit? Perhaps lay a trail of clues and wait for him to guess.

Or maybe she should stay silent on the matter for a few more weeks?

"You seem preoccupied, pet." Leo's voice interrupted her musings. "Pray tell, what has you so distracted?"

She inhaled a deep breath. It would seem the time for discussion was upon her. *Please do not let him behave as the rogue did.* "I have been thinking about going to the country," she blurted. Drat, that had come out all wrong.

Frown lines creased his forehead, and his eyes narrowed. "Whatever for?"

"I thought it might be nice… relaxing even…to get away from the city for a while." She fidgeted with the lace edging her sleeve as she strode closer to him.

"And how long would you stay in the country?" he asked.

Emeline laid her hand on his shoulder in a tender touch. She swallowed hard. Why the devil was this proving so difficult?

She blew out a slow breath. "How does nine months sound to you?"

His grey eyes turned cold like a winter sky. "You're pregnant?"

His tone froze her blood. Taken aback at his reaction, she snatched her hand away. "I expected..." He was clearly displeased, though she could not imagine why. "Yes."

Leo stood, but rather than pull her close, he retreated several steps. "Very well, then. I will have the carriage readied at first light. You can depart for Kent after breakfast."

Her heart squeezed painfully. "Me?" She laid a hand over her abdomen. "What about you?" She wanted him to come, too. To be at her side through the pregnancy and be there to greet the babe when it arrived.

She'd only meant for them to spend her confinement together. She thought he would be pleased and embrace her. Why was he so angry?

How had this conversation gone so wrong?

"What about me?" he asked, ice threaded his voice. "You have met our terms. Now you have your freedom."

He trailed his piercing stare down her body, stopping at her belly. "At least until we know if it's a boy. Should you give birth to a daughter, we will have to try again."

His words cut her to the quick. Her stomach turned queasy, and tears threatened to come.

No. No, no, no, she told herself. How dare he treat her in such away? After everything they had shared? After she had given herself so freely, heart, body, and soul.

Did he truly see her as nothing more than the woman to give birth to his heir?

"Very well, but mark my words," she pointed at him, "You will regret your actions tonight. When our child is grown and wants little to do with you, you'll have only yourself to blame. When the nights are long and the days are longer, when you desperately need comforting and companionship, but no one is about, you'll be to blame for that as well."

Gathering what remained of her dignity, she strode toward the door.

Reaching the threshold, she turned back to him. "I love you. I would have loved you forever if you'd let me."

HE'D BEEN AN ass, but there was nothing else for it. Leo could not bear to have her turn him away, so he'd done it for her.

There was less heartache when one controlled their own fate. That is what he told himself as he grabbed the brandy decanter. In truth, the words came as little comfort.

Bloody hell! He should be thrilled. She was giving him exactly what he wanted. After all, it was Leo who'd proposed this bargain. He'd been the one to insist that all she need do is produce an heir. It had been Leo who'd insisted on granting her freedom once they accomplished their goal.

Only, he'd never seen bedding her as a task. She'd proven adventurous and passionate, sweet and soft.

Emeline was unlike any woman he'd ever been with, and now that the time was upon him, bloody fool that he was, he did not wish to let her go.

'I could have loved you forever.' Her parting blow threaded through the fabric of his soul.

'Could,' that one word stung most of all. She could have loved him forever. Not that she would or did. As if loving him were a choice she could make.

In time, her memory and any longings he had for her would dissipate. He'd apply all of his energy to the estates and title. When the time came, he would groom and teach his son how to be a proper earl and carry on his legacy.

Yes, this was a happy time.

He'd gotten what he bargained for.

Romantic notions or flowery words would only lead him to ruin, and he'd have none of it.

Leo would continue on the path he'd set. He would become the most successful earl the title had ever known and pass on a powerful legacy to his son and for his people.

When thoughts of Emeline crept up, he would simply remind himself of his goals. If that failed, he'd remember what Lucinda and his brother had done to him, and how his parents had stood complacently by as his fiancé had betrayed him and fallen in love with his older brother while Leo was away at war.

The thought soured his stomach, and he knew he'd made the right choice in turning Emeline away.

Not merely the right choice, the only viable one.

CHAPTER 13

EMELINE SPENT THE nearly four-hour carriage ride from London to the Rochester countryside in Kent, pivoting between fierce anger and heartbreak.

One moment she wanted to ball up her hand and slam it into Leo's jaw, then the next minute, she was fighting tears.

His words and actions rolled through her head, and she was determined to figure him out. Nothing made sense. They had spent several glorious weeks together, and now...

How could he?

He'd all but turned her out. Sent her packing off to the country without so much as a by your leave, and with only her maid and kitten for company. He had provided three footmen for protection, though whether they were for her or the babe, she could not be certain.

The dratted man hadn't even seen her off!

Still, she refused to accept that he did not want her. There was something else going on. But what?

More importantly, how was she to discover the truth and get through to his heart while she was tucked away in the country?

Why hadn't he come with her? Did it all have to do with his family?

By the time she arrived at the country estate, she'd concluded that his odd and cold behavior must be partially due to his family. He always turned guarded when she broached the topic and never answered her queries.

She suspected something more than their deaths weighed on him, and she determined to figure out what that something was.

Emeline hoped this old manor house might hold some clues.

She had already poked around in the library and office, as well as the smoking and billiards rooms. Now she traversed a long candlelit hall on her way to the bedchambers. Maybe there would be some clue to be found in Leo's chamber?

Absurd.

She could not invade his privacy, or rather she would not. It simply wasn't the done thing. Or perhaps it was when a wife found herself desperate.

She reached for the handle of the earl's chamber and took in a deep breath. If only she had someone other than Puff to talk to. Someone like Mother to guide and help her.

Yes, she would write Mother for advice. Until then, she'd leave the earl's room as it was.

Hand shaking, she lowered it from the door, then continued to her chamber. Once her maid left her, Emeline climbed into the vast, four-post bed and sank against the feather mattress.

A hard edge pressed against her shoulder, and she winced. What on earth could it be? She rolled and stuck her hand beneath the covers, searching—the mattress hunched beneath her hand, a hard, rectangular protrusion with sharp edges greeted her. Something was beneath the mattress.

Curiosity consumed her as she left the bed, then shoved her hand between the mattress and the base of the bed.

Smooth leather met her fingertips.

She clasped her hand around the object and pulled it out. Her heart somersaulted, excitement bubbling up in her.

The mystery object was an exquisite, red leather journal with gold gilding.

Emeline opened the cover. A smile transformed her face, for this was not just any diary.

It belonged to the previous Countess of Morton.

Emeline bit the inside of her cheek and warned herself not to get too excited. The diary may hold the answers she sought, but it could just as well prove a disappointment.

She pressed her eyes closed. Please, please hold some insights.

Puff chose that moment to dart out from beneath the bed and swat at her hands. Emeline nearly dropped the diary as she jerked away from his sharp claws.

"Stop that," she scolded, lifting her hands along with the diary out of the kitten's reach. "Lay down," she added.

To her surprise, Puff curled up on the carpet beside her and began to purr.

"Good kitty," she said as she sank back on her heels, she turned to the next page.

Hours passed as she flipped page by page, searching for something that would help her understand Leo. Thus far, all of the entries were pleasant. Certainly, nothing unexpected. The countess wrote about her sons, hopes, dreams, and her husband.

It proved riveting but did little to answer Emeline's many questions.

Emeline formed the image of a happy and affluent family as she read. They attended balls and picnics, entertained guests, and hosted house parties—all the things one would expect of an aristocratic family. The date was now eighteen-twelve, and the countess wrote of the war.

'It both gladdens and saddens my heart to think of my brave boy

going off to fight. I worry for his safety as any mother would, but admire his bravery and dedication to the cause.'

A line further down the entry caused her breath to catch.

'There is joy in the face of uncertainty as Leo and Lucinda are now betrothed. When my Leo returns, there will be a grand wedding to celebrate.'

Good heavens, he'd been engaged! Emeline's mind spun with questions. Who was Lucinda? What had prevented their marriage? Did it have something to do with his current behavior? With the way he had sent her off?

Several pages later, another entry caught her attention.

'My dear Leonard left to join his regiment today. Poor Lucinda is beside herself. I, too, have sobbed myself dry with missing him and worrying over his safety. My sweet, sweet Harold came to me a little while ago. He held me and spoke words of comfort. Harold reminded me that our boys, both Leo and Georgie, are strong and smart. He's right, of course. I shall have to remind myself often that Leo is well prepared for his role as a soldier and take comfort in the fact that I still have Georgie at home. I trust that the good Lord will return Leo to me as well.'

Emeline released a breath she hadn't known she was holding. Her heart ached for the pain and uncertainty that Leo's mother had felt.

One thing was abundantly clear to Emeline; the countess had loved her son a great deal.

It seemed that the lot of them had loved each other immensely. Perhaps their bond was so great, their kinship so deeply rooted, that Leo simply could not bring himself to speak of them now that they were gone?

Maybe he was afraid to love again because the pain of losing them was so great?

What could she do to get through to him? Surely there was a way to help him. Something she could do to convince him to take a chance on her. But what?

She brought her hand to her mouth to cover a yawn. The hour was now well past midnight, and her eyes had grown heavy.

Clutching the diary to her chest, she settled back onto the bed. A few more pages, then she would sleep.

'My heart is forever broken. What is a mother to do when she has no way of protecting those she loves? That is the situation I now face. Lady Lucinda came to me in tears today. The poor dear had nowhere else to turn. With red-rimmed eyes, she confessed that she and Leo had anticipated their vows.

She's with child. My grandchild!

She begged me to help her as she couldn't possibly tell her parents and has nowhere else to turn. We have no way of getting word to Leo. Even if we could, he is at war. My dearest, foolish boy cannot abandon his regiment.

Harold and George joined us in the parlor. At first, Harold was furious. How could the two of them be so stupid? He'd asked as he paced the room. Their actions would leave them all ruined, and the child, our grandchild, would be a bastard.

By that time, I was sobbing beside Lucinda, feeling every bit as lost and distraught as she. We could not allow for such an outcome. The poor dear did not deserve ruination. This was Leo's child, and it should bear his name. But with Leo so far away and unreachable, how could that happen?'

Emeline lowered one hand to her belly. Her eyes stung with unshed tears. Poor Lucinda, she could not imagine how distraught the lady must have been.

Emeline dashed the tears from her cheeks and began to read once again.

That is when George proposed he marry her in Leo's absence. He could claim the child and raise it as his own. They would all be saved. Leo would be furious, but in the end, he would come to forgive them.

No. I had protested. I refuse to be a party to breaking my son's heart. We cannot betray him while he is off defending king and country.

Lucinda agreed. She wailed harder, her tears cascading down her cheeks. "I love Leo. I have to wait for him. There must be another way." It broke all of us and the impossible situation we now face.'

By diary's end, Emeline found the answers she sought. Not only had Lucinda married Leo's brother, but a sennight after they'd said their vows, she lost the baby.

Emeline sat the diary aside, then picked Puff up and nuzzled her face against his soft fur. She muttered, "It was all for naught."

The kitten mewed and wriggled free of her hold.

She dried her eyes, then blew out the candle. Poor Leo had suffered a great deal. He needed love and comfort, though she now knew that he would never ask for it.

Those he'd loved most had hurt him deeply. Trust would not come easy for him now.

Worse, she would wager her soul that he did not know why Lucinda and George had married.

How could he when they all died before he returned?

She would go to him tomorrow. Take him the diary and insist he read it.

Better yet, she would read it to him. She would make sure he learned the truth. He deserved that much. Even if he still didn't want her. Even if his heart would never be free to love again, he needed to hear the truth.

And she would see that he did.

CHAPTER 14

NEVER HAD LEO endured a more painful and sleepless night. He'd tossed and turned for hours, rising many times in between so he could down tumblers of whiskey.

Not even the liquor helped.

He could not drink enough to stop missing Emeline, nor could he get drunk enough to sleep. Nothing could save him now.

He knew this feeling all too well.

Emeline had his heart.

His fool heart belonged to her. Despite his resistance, he'd fallen in love with his wife.

He made the startling discovery in the wee morning hours before the sun crested the horizon.

For long moments, Leo stared out his bedchamber window at the inky sky and fading stars, a forgotten tumbler of whisky clutched in his hand. Devil take it, he loved her.

And he'd cast her out. Pushed her away. Broken her tender heart.

He shook his head at the realization.

He'd been a bloody jackass.

The fear of being betrayed again had ruled his mind and actions.

He'd foolishly believed he could forget her.

'I love you. I could have loved you forever if you'd let me.' Her words pierced his thoughts.

Hope bloomed in his heart. Could she still love him forever? Would she forgive him?

He had to go to her. Plead his case. Beg forgiveness.

Leo had to redeem himself. Had to fix what he had broken. If there was even the smallest of chances that she could love him, he had to go to her.

Thirty miles separated them.

If he took his stallion, he could reach her in under six hours. That would have him at her side shortly after sunrise.

He departed for Kent the moment his mount was ready.

Mile after mile passed, a cloud of dust trailing behind him.

Many hours later, he slowed his stallion and smoothed his hand down the beast's neck.

He hadn't been here since he discovered how his family and Lucinda had betrayed him. Old hurts squeezed his chest. He would never understand how his betrothed could have married his brother or how George could have betrayed him. The fact that his parents stood by without protest cut even deeper.

Their actions no longer signified.

They were all gone from this world. Emeline was here, and he loved her. Bloody hell, he would not allow the past to cause more trouble than it already had. It was behind him, and that is where it would stay from this moment forward. From now on, he would look straight ahead to his future with his wife.

God willing, she would still have him.

"Just a little further," he soothed the horse before nudging it back into a gallop.

His heart thudded when he turned down the long drive to find his carriage parked out front.

Footmen piled the top with trunks, hatboxes, and bags stuck out of the boot. His throat tightened. She was leaving him.

He would not let her go. Not now. He couldn't.

Determined to have his say, he jumped from his mount and ran into the house.

Startled, his butler jumped out of the way. "My lord, we were not expecting you."

"Clearly," Leo ground out before casting his glance around the entry hall. "Where is my wife?"

"She has yet to come down, my lord. I believe she is in her chamber."

Leo wasted no more time on the butler. He marched across the entry hall, took the stairs, then traversed the hallway with long, quick strides.

He'd come this far; nothing would stop him now.

Nothing but Emeline.

"Leo."

He pivoted, his heart in his throat. She stood before him, clad in a traveling gown. Her chin slanted at a delicate angle as she studied him. "What are you doing here?"

He flinched at the edge in her tone. She was displeased, and she had every right to be.

"Leo." She arched one delicate eyebrow.

"I came for you," he said.

A smile transformed her face as she started toward him. "I was on my way to you."

Emeline cupped his face and stared into his eyes. "I have something I must show you. There are things you must know that I am quite certain you do not."

Her words piqued his curiosity. What could she be on about?

Before he could say anything, she took his arm and pulled him into her bedchamber. A knot formed in his stomach as he watched her reach into the valise resting on her bed. His heart ceased to beat when she pulled out his mother's diary.

He would recognize that blasted book anywhere.

Mother had written in it faithfully every night. As a lad, he had often played nearby as she recorded her thoughts for the day. Each time she filled one, Father would present her with another.

Every single one had the same red leather binding and gold gilded design.

He swallowed past the dryness in his mouth and willed his pounding heart to calm. It was only a book.

The traitor's diary, his mind screamed.

No, he told himself, *do not get dissuaded*. That book was the past. He was here for the future.

"I read it last night," Emeline said. "I know about Lucinda. I know everything."

Bile rose in his throat. He pulled the diary from her hand and turned and pitched it out the open window.

She gasped. "Leo!" Emeline ran to the open window and peered out. "It's landed in a puddle of water and is likely ruined. Why did you do that?" She turned on him, her eyes wide. "You don't understand."

"On the contrary, pet. I understand perfectly." He closed the distance between them. "And I hope they are all burning in hell."

She had the good sense not to flinch and held her ground. "You do not mean that."

"Of course I do. She married my brother. My parents gave their blessing. They all betrayed me."

"She was pregnant," Emeline argued.

"With his child." Fresh anger burned through him.

"No," Emeline said. "The babe—"

He dipped his head and captured her lips. His mouth moving against hers in a bruising kiss meant to distract. The tactic failed.

She pushed against his chest, pulling her lips from his. "Don't do that."

"What?" he asked. "This?" And he pulled her back into his arms, desperate to hold her. Desperate to forget.

She turned her head away. "Leo, I'm serious. You must hear the truth."

"I know the truth, and it has nothing to do with us."

"It has everything to do with us," she protested. "You are hurting, and because of it, you continue to push me away."

He changed tactics, released her, and strode to the hearth.

After drawing in a deep breath, he pivoted back to her. "Emeline, I love you. I came here to beg your forgiveness. To admit to you, I was a jackass for sending you here alone. I came to offer my heart, and I came hoping I still had yours."

He looked away. "I don't care about the past. I want a future with you."

"Oh, Leo." She drew close to him and laid her hand on his arm. "I want that, too."

He turned his gaze to her, searching her warm brown eyes. "Then let me love you. Be my countess, my friend, and my lover for the rest of our days."

Emeline nodded. "I want nothing more."

His heart warmed, all the anger that had been surging through him melted away.

She forgave him.

This caring, sweet, vivacious, and intelligent woman loved him.

"Let me show you how much I love you." He stroked his finger down her chest. "I'm going to make love to you past dusk and well into the night."

Her gaze filled with desire as she stared back at him, her lips parted, and her breaths came heavier. "Only if you let me love you back. Today, tonight, and always," she said, her voice husky.

CHAPTER 15

EMELINE'S BODY HUMMED with pleasure as she lay snuggled against Leo. He had indeed loved her for hours, bringing her to rapture time and again.

He'd explored every inch of her with his hands, tongue, and wicked fingers. He'd kissed deeply, passionately as he thrust in and out of her. When she cried out with pleasure, he drowned the moans with kisses, and when they were spent, he held her close, making no effort to flee her bed.

This was everything she'd wanted. Everything save for one monumental thing. He could not love her fully as long as the past continued to eat away at him.

Hadn't her own past taught her as much? And the emotional scars on her soul were not nearly as profound as his.

He may say he didn't care, but she knew the truth. Leo cared deeply. Perhaps if he knew the truth, he could forgive them. Then he could heal, and they could share the life they both longed for.

She blew a stray curl away from her eye, then stroked her fingers over his chest. "Do you love me?"

"I do," he said. "With all I have to give."

She swallowed. "I want more. I want everything, including your trust." She lifted up to meet his gaze. "Can you grant me everything?"

Leo pressed his eyes closed. "You are not going to let this go, are you?"

"I cannot, for if I did, you would never be whole. *We* would never be whole." She dropped a kiss to his chest. "I love you completely, Leo. You can trust me."

He opened his eyes to find her staring at him, her gaze pleading.

"Let me tell you what happened."

"I already—"

She placed two fingers over his mouth, quieting him. "You do not know everything. I am as sure of it as I am that the sun will rise tomorrow. There is no way you could know the full story."

"I only need to know that you love me, Emeline. That you will never betray me," he slid his hand to her belly, "or our children."

"I wouldn't dream of it," she said. "And neither did your mother."

He groaned as he pressed his head back against the pillows.

She found his actions encouraging, for he'd not bothered to argue or hush her, and so she continued. "When Lucinda married George, she was carrying your child. Your mother wrote all about it."

Leo's gaze narrowed.

"It is true, Leo. She confessed that the two of you anticipated your vows. Do you deny it?" Emeline rested her hand on his cheek, forcing him to hold her gaze.

"No," he ground out the word.

"Then, you must also believe that she was terrified and alone. There was no way to reach you, and, according to your mother, even if they could send word, you would not have been able to leave your regiment."

She waited, her heart pounding forcefully. He needed time. Time to absorb the truth. Time to speak. He only stared at her, emotions passing through his eyes like summer storms.

"She would have been ruined, Leo. Your child would have been born a bastard. He or she would have been ostracized and ridiculed or hidden away from the world. None of them wanted that. They did not believe you would have wanted that either. Don't you understand, they didn't see any other choice. Marriage was the only way to save Lucinda and your babe. They did the best they could, given the circumstances."

Emeline attempted to get up, but Leo tightened his arms around her. "Let me go. Perhaps it is not too late to save the diary."

She'd seen it floating in the puddle below. By now, the pages were likely soaked through, and the ink smeared. But she had to take the chance. Leo needed to read his mother's words for himself. Perhaps then, he would see the sorrow she'd experienced and understand how helpless they had all felt.

"No," he said, pulling her closer. "I have no need of it."

Good heavens, he was fighting tears.

She brushed her hand over his brow, smoothed the hair from his forehead. "Let it out, my love. Grieve, rage, do what you must. I won't judge you."

Then he broke. Leo buried his head in her lap and quietly sobbed.

Emeline could scarcely guess how much time passed as she held him. She stroked her fingers through his hair, over his back, and whispering tender phrases meant to soothe as he cried.

At last, he turned his red-rimmed gaze to her. "I love you."

Emeline smiled down at him. "I love you, too."

"Thank you for discovering the truth," he said, "and for making me hear it. Most of all, thank you for holding tight to me when any other woman would have given up. I don't deserve you, pet, but I vow to spend the rest of my life loving you despite it."

They spent the rest of the night talking about the past, present, and future. She told him about the rogue. He told her about Lucinda.

When they grew tired of talking, they made love or held each other in companionable silence. By first light, no secrets remained between them.

He stared into her eyes and said, "You have all of me now. Heart, body, and soul."

Emeline stared boldly back at him. "And you have all of me."

EPILOGUE

Five years later

A WARM SUMMER breeze blew across the family cemetery as Leo laid a wildflower bouquet on his mother's grave. He placed his hand on the cold marble stone that bore her name.

He and Emeline had first come here five years ago today. It was the morning after she'd told him about the diary. The first day of the rest of their lives.

She'd held his hand as he'd forgiven them all. Then together, they had collected flowers and laid them on the graves.

His forgiving and generous wife had even paid her respects to Lucinda. The act had freed Leo's heart from the pains of the past and brought him and Emeline closer.

Every year thereafter, the two of them, along with their children, visited the family cemetery on this day. It was their tradition and one more reason why he loved his wife.

Not that he needed another reason. She was his everything and always would be.

He turned his smile on her as he took their daughter, Mary's, hand. "Shall we return to the house now?" He called to where Emeline stood, holding their son, George.

She rested her free hand over the swell of her belly. They were expecting their third child by summer's end. If it were a boy, they would name him Harold after his father.

"I want to pick more flowers, Daddy," Mary protested.

Emeline strode toward them. "That will have to wait, darling." George wailed, his cries shattering the peaceful afternoon. "I'm afraid your brother is growing impatient."

Mary's face twisted up in disgust. "I don't want any more brothers." She turned her gaze on Leo. "Can we have a girl this time."

Leo scooped Mary into his arms, drawing her close. "What is so wrong with having another brother?"

Mary sighed as she turned to look at George. "He cries too much and stinks more often than not."

Emeline laughed as she nuzzled their son.

Leo chuckled as he bounced his daughter in his arms. She had the right of it. At only seventeen-months of age, her brother was short on words and high on smells.

Emeline grinned at Leo before turning her attention to Mary. "Give him time, darling. Soon he will be big enough to play with you. And I promise he won't stink."

"Is that true, Daddy?"

"You can always trust your mama," he said, then shared a silent exchange with Emeline. "Never doubt it, poppet."

"Very well," Mary said as she wrapped her arms about Leo's neck and rested her small face against his shoulder. "I suppose we should return home then."

Emeline reached for Leo's hand as he drew near, then they started back toward the house.

Mary popped her head up as they strolled past George and Lucinda's graves. "What will we name her if she is a sister?" she asked, glancing between Leo and Emeline.

Leo swallowed, not sure how to answer. Mary shared her name with his mother, and they had named George after his brother. If they had another son, they would name him for Leo's father, but a daughter... Surely not.

"She should be named Lucinda," Mary said. "It is the only girl's name left." She turned her attention to the row of marble stones. "We can call her Lucy."

Leo swallowed hard. He would never ask Emeline to honor the name of—

"It is as if you read my mind, little one," Emeline said, her tone cheery.

Mary smiled with pride. "Then it is settled. We shall have a girl, and I will call her Lucy."

Leo's heart swelled with love and pride. Emeline was the kindest and most generous person he'd ever known, and he would never forget how lucky he was to have found her.

Still, he could not let her agree to such a thing. It wasn't right. He slanted his gaze to her. "There are many other names to choose from. Perhaps, Olivia? That was Mother's middle name."

"Nonsense." Emeline waved her hand in dismissal. "Lucinda is a fine name. I would be happy to use it." She smiled at him. "I'd be pleased to honor her."

Leo's throat tightened and squeezed her hand in silent confirmation. There was no need for words, for he knew without a doubt that she understood him as no other ever could.

"I will love you forever, too," she said.

And he had no doubt she would.

About Amanda Mariel

USA Today Bestselling author Amanda Mariel dreams of days gone by when life moved at a slower pace. She enjoys taking pen to paper and exploring historical time periods through her imagination and the written word. When she is not writing she can be found reading, crocheting, traveling, practicing her photography skills, or spending time with her family.

Visit www.amandamariel.com to learn more about Amanda and her books. Sign up for Amanda's newsletter while you are on her website to stay up-to-date on all things Amanda Mariel and receive a free eBook!

Text **AmandaMariel** to **38470** to be notified by SMS/text message *ONLY* when there is a new release or book sale. Bonus: Receive a free eBook when you subscribe!! **At this time SMS/text notifications are only available in the US and Canada**

Amanda loves to hear from her fans! Email her at amanda@amandamariel.com or find her on social media:

Facebook:
facebook.com/AuthorAmandaMariel

Twitter:
twitter.com/AmandaMarieAuth

BookBub:
bookbub.com/authors/amanda-mariel

Instagram:
instagram.com/authoramandamariel

Thank you so much for taking the time to read A Lyon in Her Bed.

Your opinion matters!

Please take a moment to review this book on your favorite review site and share your opinion with fellow readers.

USA Today bestselling author

~Heartwarming historical romances that leave you breathless~